Born Rotten
(A Married in Malibu Novella)

BORN ROTTEN

A Married in Malibu Novella

KAILIN GOW

AUTHOR'S NOTE

Thank you for picking up Born Rotten.

This series is a romance recommended for age 17 and up.

Chapter 1

<u>Dex</u>

Age 18

Early on in my life, I knew I was trouble. My drug addict mother who died when I was 13, always drilled it into my head that I was born rotten.

Not long after my eighteenth birthday, I got a doozy of a birthday gift. A good and solid beating by a few of the neighborhood gang members from Santa Ana, a city south of Los Angeles, California.

Three of them had ganged up on me.

"Where you going, Halliwell?" Hector said.

"Just going home, man."

"This isn't the way to your place," Mark said.

"Hey, man," I said. "It's a free country. The streets belong to everyone."

"Not in this neighborhood," Alex said.

I knew these guys were rough and they enjoyed intimidating anyone who dared cross into their territory.

"My bad, dude," I said, taking a step back. "I'll go and take…"

"Too late now, Halliwell," Mark said. "The damage is done."

He pushed me back against a chain link fence then punched me in the gut, taking me by surprise. I doubled over and got another punch in the face, this time from Alex.

"Hey. Don't leave me out," Hector said as he stepped between them and gave me a double whammy. A right fist to the nose and a left to the jaw.

I was on the verge of blacking out. My legs turned to jelly, and I crumbled to the ground.

Born Rotten
(A Married in Malibu Novella)

"Get the message, Halliwell?" Alex said, giving me a kick in the gut just for good measure.

Spitting up blood, I doubled over, trying to protect myself from another strike.

"Better remember for next time," Hector said. "Or the next time will be your last time."

They walked away but I remained on the ground for nearly fifteen minutes. Part of me was afraid they'd come back. Another part of me wondered if I'd even be able to stand upright.

Clinging to the fence, I pulled myself up and leaned against it for a minute. Finally feeling sure on my feet, I headed home to my aunt's house.

"Aunt Donna," I called as I walked into the dirty and unkept house.

I kicked aside the empty box of cat litter that had been lying in the hallway for over a week. Three cats scrambled out of my way as I entered the living room and found Aunt Donna passed out on the sofa. Nothing unusual here.

"I guess there's no point in asking you what's for dinner," I said as I swiped the back of my hand over my bloody mouth.

I went to the bathroom, cleared the sink of dirty tissues, a hairbrush overflowing with long blond hair and a rusty flat iron. Then I ran the cold water and splashed it over my face.

Looking in the mirror, I asked myself for the hundredth time what I was doing there.

Oh yeah, it was because the court awarded her custody of me as my only relative. Not that she wanted me. Maybe a foster home would have been better, but the court didn't think so.

How had my life become so goddamned shitty?

If I wasn't being told that I was stupid by a teacher, I was getting beat up by thugs, and when that wasn't enough, I had my dear old aunt there to make me feel so at home. It was a miracle I haven't joined one of the gangs yet and ended up dead or in

Born Rotten
(A Married in Malibu Novella)

Juvie behind bars. No thanks to my aunt. Like I said, it was a miracle I was still alive.

Right. She treated her cats better than she treated me.

"To hell with this," I said as I wiped my face on the cleanest towel I could find.

I was now of age. Legally an adult at eighteen years old.

"Happy Birthday to me," I muttered to myself.

I went back to the living room which served as my bedroom and found my car keys on the coffee table.

"See you later… Auntie."

I headed out to my beat-up old car and hoped it would start. It'd been giving me a headache lately, but I couldn't afford to have it fixed.

I put the key in the ignition and prayed. It coughed. It chugged and coughed again. Then, the sound I was hoping for. A thundering roar as it started. Taking it easy on the road, I drove around and ended up on Interstate 5 heading west.

Where to? I asked myself.

Does it matter?

I drove on and headed into Irvine, the closest city near Santa Ana that was as nice as a city I can imagine.

The change of pace was good. The change of scenery was good.

Just a change… anything was good.

I pulled up in front of a large church. Somehow it seemed welcoming. I wasn't a religious guy… not in the slightest. Yet on that day… There was something that called to me.

I parked the car and got out, walking around the grounds under the shade of huge leafy trees. In the distance I noticed a girl, a real geek, walk out of the church and head to the base of one of the trees.

She sat down, as if this was her usual routine. She seemed so comfortable and at peace. Out of her shoulder bag, she pulled a notepad and proceeded to write.

Mesmerized by her, I sat down on a bench to watch her. She wrote and wrote and wrote until I longed to know what she was writing about.

What was it about her? She was just a geek. Totally not my type. Totally the opposite of my type.

Then why can't you stop looking at her?

Who the hell knows?

Maybe a little envy. Maybe this is the big change that I need.

What if…?

What if I could make that change?

I looked up at the church. I jotted down the address. On my way to the church, I had noticed a large high school. Nice, clean… peaceful.

Yeah, I thought again. What if…?

It's worth a try.

I found the phone number to the school and called.

"Irvine High," a nasally voice said. "I'm Iris Gooby. Education is our priority. How can I help you?"

"Hello," I said. "I just moved into town and need to transfer."

"All right," she said. "Where are you transferring from?"

"Santa Ana."

"And when would you be ready to start here at Irvine?"

"Right away," I said. "Tomorrow."

"That's a little last minute, isn't it?"

"The move came rather unexpectedly," I said.

"All right. Your name?"

"Dex Halliwell."

"Your address?"

I looked around until I saw the street sign near the church and then the number of the building the girl had just walked out of. I gave her the church's address and hoped she wouldn't realize it was a church.

"Okay," she said as she jotted it down. "Well, Mr. Halliwell. I'll make the call to get your records from Santa Ana, although I will need your parents' permission."

"I don't have any parents."

"Guardian?"

"I'm eighteen," I said, putting an end to that line of questioning.

"Very well," she said. "You can come in tomorrow morning at ten o'clock and meet with Principal Chen."

"Does that mean that I'm enrolled?"

"Just be here tomorrow at ten."

"Thank you."

I ended the call and turned to see the geeky girl still sitting there under the tree… writing.

Maybe one day, if all goes well in this new school, I'll enjoy an afternoon breeze and sit beneath a tree writing, too, enjoying some peace.

That night, I parked on a quiet street near the school and slept in my car.

First thing the next morning, I headed to the school and was led to the principal's office.

"Mr. Halliwell," Principal Chen said as she invited me to sit down. "It's always a pleasure to have a new student in our midst."

"It's nice to be here," I said.

She looked at the computer screen on her desk. "While we're pleased to have you here, I see here that you're having difficulties in several subjects."

"Yeah," I said. "Things have been a little rough at home these days. But I fully intend to get those grades up."

"I appreciate that, but I'm afraid you're going to have to get them up a little faster than you might think."

Born Rotten
(A Married in Malibu Novella)

"Oh?"

She nodded. "I've taken the liberty of calling on one of our best students to come meet you. I believe she'll be able to get your grades to where they need to be."

"Oh," I muttered, kind of disappointed.

"She should be here any minute now."

She? I didn't want no 'she' teaching me what I didn't know.

Come to think of it, I didn't really want a 'he' teaching me anything either. I just wanted to sit in a class with other students and learn with everyone else.

A knock sounded at the door. "It's Taylor Rhee."

"And there she is now," Principal Chen said. "Come in."

As the door opened, I looked up to see this genius tutor… this Taylor Rhee.

Holy shit, I thought when I saw her. It was the same girl that I'd seen at the church the day before. That geeky girl who sat under the tree. Her hair had been in two side ponytails, giving her an innocent little girl look, but up close, she had big doe-like brown eyes, high cheekbones, a cute nose, and full lips.

She was so pretty that makeup would ruin her beauty. Different from all the girls I've known before at my old school, instantly my guard was up.

Chapter 2

<u>Taylor</u>

Age 18

If I'd known my life was going to change today, I would have stayed in bed. I didn't need the distraction. I didn't need anything that would take me off my goals.

"Congratulations, Taylor," my AP Biology teacher Mr. Maxwell said. "You got the highest score as usual."

"Thank you," I said as he handed me the test. I turned to walk out.

"Oh," Mr. Maxwell called after me. "Principal Chen would like to see you."

Me? Why would the principal want to see me?

"Okay," I said. "Thank you."

As I walked to the principal's office, I tried to guess why I'd been called. I was a good student. I wasn't a troublemaker. It didn't make any sense.

I reached the office and knocked.

"Who is it?"

"Taylor Rhee."

"Come in."

I opened the door to find Principal Chen behind her desk, her thin face looking up at me. I then noticed the dark-haired boy sitting in one of the chairs facing her.

He glared up at me from under his long bangs that partially obscured his face. His hazel eyes held a world of intrigue, but the hard glare left me fidgeting uncomfortably as I sat down in the chair beside him.

I tried to concentrate on Principal Chen, but my eyes returned to the angry young man. Like a magnet, he drew me in, made me curious and had me wanting to know more.

Born Rotten
(A Married in Malibu Novella)

The tattoos on his arms told a part of the story. A bad boy who was into realistic images that gave the impression of a snake weaving in and out of his skin on one arm, and robotic mechanisms under the skin of the other. His ears donned large black pearls and his upper lip was pierced and adorned with a silver ring.

"Taylor," Principal Chen said. "This is Dex Halliwell."

I glanced at him again and pressed an unsure smile. He responded with a sneer.

"He just transferred here from Santa Ana High."

"Oh. How nice," I said, wondering wildly what all of this had to do with me.

All the while, my body was raging with its own confusion. He was clearly a bad boy in every sense of the word and the last type of guy that should appeal to me.

And yet, there it was. My body tingled and the more he glared at me, the more I tingled. Sure he was hot. Probably the hottest guy I've ever seen in school. Sexy, rebellious, grumpy… completely my opposite. Completely wrong for me.

"Dex needs to be brought up to speed, as it were," Principal Chen said. "He has several subjects that he needs to catch up on, or he'll be repeating his twelfth grade."

I nodded and waited for her to go on.

"Taylor Rhee is one of the smartest girls here," she told Dex. "And she is undoubtedly the smartest person you'll ever meet."

He grunted.

"She's also a sweetheart of a girl who is funny and kind in addition to being brilliant. A sunshine of a girl."

Another grunt.

"So, I do hope you'll be a gentleman and not corrupt her."

Born Rotten
(A Married in Malibu Novella)

He gave me a chilly up and down glare, then sneered with disdain.

"After all, she's probably the only person who can help you with your grades, so I trust that you'll be nice and respectful."

"Don't worry," the brooding hot guy said as he shot me another disgusted glare. "I won't do her."

"Dex!" Principal Chen said. "Watch your mouth."

He groaned.

"Taylor," she said, turning to me. "I do apologize. You see, Dex is from…"

"Don't worry about it," I said, sending the arrogant bad boy a disdainful glare of my own. "If what you say is true, he needs me more than I need him. If he wants my help, he'll learn to watch his mouth. I'll teach him some manners."

"Pretty confident for a little squeak of a girl."

"Spoken like a real man," I said sarcastically.

"You're not the first to be enlisted to supposedly *help me*," he said, putting air quotes on 'help me'. "They've all failed. I don't see how you could do any better."

"You got any other options?" I shot at him.

He shrugged and sneered as he flipped his bangs out of his face, only to have the thick dark hair fall back where it had been. "You think you're pretty special, don't you? Well, you're not. You're just another goody-goody dogface who can't get any action. When's the last time you spent time with a guy, huh?"

I stared at him in stunned silence. What did that have to do with anything?

"Yeah… that's what I thought," he went on. "You've never put your head down any guy's crotch, have you?"

"Dex!" Principal Chen said.

"So why don't you go back to your studies and stick your dogface little head in your books," Dex said.

Born Rotten
(A Married in Malibu Novella)

"Dex!" Principal Chen shouted. "That's enough."

"Heh," he grunted.

"You give me no choice but to put you in detention after school."

"Whatever."

Principal Chen looked at me. "I'm so sorry that Dex is being so unreceptive. I think he's making a grave mistake with this attitude. You don't have to do this if you don't want to."

"Oh, please," Dex said as he leaned back and glared up at the ceiling. "Don't make me spend a minute with this eyesore. I'd rather have detention and just stare at a blank wall for an hour."

My jaw tightened as I glanced sidelong at him. What was with all the insults? Okay, so I was not a fashionista like Britney or Lydia. I was petite and athletic instead of curvaceous, and my long black hair just lay there or was sometimes pulled into a ponytail or side ponytails.

But still... I was far from deserving such venom.

"Man," he muttered as he looked at me again. "You couldn't pay me enough to do her. Look at her. Who would ever want to touch her?" He shuddered and made a disgusted face. "Probably one of the ugliest dogfaces I've ever seen."

A painful ball of emotions lodged itself in my throat as I fought the tears that were threatening to well up in my eyes. Damn if I was going to give him the satisfaction of actually hurting my feelings.

After all, who was he? Just some loser who was probably going to wind up in prison the moment he left school.

He leaned over the arm of his chair suddenly and barked in my face. Startled, I jumped back, but quickly regained my composure.

"Fine," I said as I stood and looked down at him. "Fail all your classes, you little dickwad! When you go on a crime spree because that useless brain of yours can't get you a job, you'll wind up in prison while I'll be making a few hundred grand a year treating patients. See if I give a fuck what happens to you."

"Boo hoo," Dex said, but I could tell that I'd nicked his ego a bit.

"Ooh… and such biting repartee," I said. "No wonder you hide behind all that hair. I'd be embarrassed too if I were you. Hell, you're just all smack talk and a shitty attitude."

He gripped the arms of the chair and stared directly in front of him.

"Don't waste your energy feeling sorry for me, bad boy. Feel sorry for yourself, because you have a long and miserable life ahead of you."

I turned to head to the door and looked back at the principal. "Thank you for the offer, Mrs. Chen, but I'll respectfully decline. You'll have to find someone else to tutor Mr. Halliwell. I have better things to do with my time… like scrub my toilet."

I opened the door and rushed out, eager to get as far away from that office as I could. I marched down the hall, oblivious of those that I passed on my way out the main door of the school.

I was shaken and I hated it. I didn't want that silly boy to get to me.

But damn. He did.

I hated how I'd been so instantly drawn to him, to that dangerous and brooding glare.

But, oh my. My body still tingled at the thought of him.

As I walked through the parking lot and glanced at my reflection in the car windows, I couldn't help but see me through his eyes.

Dogface.

I sighed. Would I ever blossom, as my mother had promised? Would I ever be able to measure up to all the perfect girls who roamed the halls of the school? The beautifully-made up faces and designer clothes the Britneys of the school wore. And all the perfection that was on display in every magazine, in every television show, in every movie?

Images of perfect women were all around me, and it all left me feeling increasingly small and insignificant.

Chapter 3

<u>Dex</u>

That goody goody girl Taylor Rhee was the least of my worries. Sure, she was cute, and I would do her, no doubt. She had a desirable body underneath those plain clothes, but I wasn't in the mood to think about that. Well, not too much. Right now I have real worries.

Had she seen me at the church before? Did she know that I was essentially homeless? If she knew I was using the church's address as my address for the school, would she rat me out?

I couldn't go back to Santa Ana where Hector and his gang was waiting for me. I couldn't go back to that life. It was vicious and dirty, nothing like what this goody two-shoes would know anything about. Nothing anyone at this new school or this neighborhood would know.

My protective wall immediately went up. I knew how the game was played. Be tough and get the upper hand or get trampled on.

I sneered at her. I criticized her. I insulted her. What else could I do? I couldn't very well shake her hand and say, 'Oh, yeah. I saw you sitting under a tree yesterday in front of the church.' 'Oh, I live there now. Yeah. In the church. Or rather in my car that is parked near the church.'

Damn, I felt like such a loser.

Maybe transferring out to Irvine wasn't such a good idea after all. But what fucking choice did I have? Go back to Santa Ana and get my ass kicked every day… or worse. Shit, I knew those guys. Hector and his gang. Next time they saw me they'd probably kill me.

When she wasn't looking, I sneaked a peek at the girl beside me and wondered what her biggest worry in the world was. Was she afraid for her life every time she walked to school? Did she have to eat crackers for lunch and simply explain to her friends that she wasn't really hungry? Did she go around stealing small pouches of ketchup to put on those crackers?

No. Probably not.

And she probably didn't have to wash her clothes every other day because she had no other clothes to wear.

Nope. Not a worry there either… hey, little Einstein? Her shoes, while far from the height of fashion, looked new. She wore simple jeans, not too snug, but just enough to give me a glimpse of her trim figure. Over that she wore a loose-fitting pink t-shirt.

Not designer clothes like some of the girls I've seen walking the halls of the Irvine High School, but still nice and new plain clothes on an otherwise well-groomed and neat girl. Too neat and tidy for me. Definitely not my type. I like them wild, loose, and easy… the kind whom I can get down and dirty with for a short while, then forget about as soon as it's over.

She glanced at me as Principal Chen spoke and I grimaced, letting her know just how unappealing I found her.

And yet… there was something in the way she looked at me. Like I was actually a person. Like maybe she might want to help me out.

But what the hell did I care? No way was I going to let her see inside of me.

Remember Hector's gang, a little voice at the back of my mind said.

Fuck him.

But then the little chit of a girl had had enough of my tough guy act. Shouting insults back at me she stood up. She definitely has some fire in her. A streak that, if stroke, would be very interesting to watch.

Shit. Now I'd really done it. My one chance to come to this new school and I'd ruined it.

I was such a fucking idiot.

After she walked out, Principal Chen pursed her lips and looked at me with a disapproving glare.

"Are you happy now?" she said.

I shrugged.

"You really think you can get your grades up to where they need to be on your own?"

I shrugged again.

"Mr. Halliwell," she said. "I really think that you're getting off on the wrong foot here."

I stared straight in front of me.

"Mr. Halliwell?"

If I went back to Santa Ana… Hector and his gang had already tried to recruit me. They'd talked tough about initiation… a kill.

Hell. There was no way I was going to kill someone just to prove to those losers that I was tough enough to be one of them.

So you'll let them kill you instead?

Born Rotten
(A Married in Malibu Novella)

And now you're back to those choices, that little voice in my head said.

"I can talk to Miss Rhee and apologize on your behalf," Principal Chen said. "I'll let her know that you're just shaken up by the change in school. If you promise to treat that girl with respect, I'll make sure she takes you on as a private student."

Sneering, I chewed on my inner cheek for a moment. I had no choice. No matter how I looked at it, I had no fucking choice.

I nodded. "Tell her I'm sorry."

Chapter 4

<u>Dex</u>

I sat on a bench in front of the church waiting for her. For whatever stupid reason, I felt nervous. Shit, I never felt nervous… not even when Hector was on my back.

But then I saw her coming up the walkway. The sun hit her dark hair, so silky and smooth. It flowed behind her, picking up on the breeze.

She wore the jeans as the day before, but with a short, slightly more form fitting dark pink t-shirt.

Nice feminine figure, I thought. Tempting, round breasts that were firm and inviting. A tiny little waist that I could probably wrap my hands around. And… when she turned to wave at a friend who passed by on the sidewalk behind her, she offered me a pleasing view of her nicely rounded ass. I pictured her naked, and my dick twitched with interest.

No. I'm not interested in her that way.
Yeah, right.

She really wasn't all that bad after all. Maybe just a little too smart for my liking. Just a little too sweet and innocent. Just a little too…

Naked and horny?
Fuck no!

"Mr. Halliwell," she said as she reached me.

"You can call me *Dex*," I said, trying to switch off my dick and act like the gentleman that Principal Chen had told me to be.

"I was told that you were having trouble in English, Math and…" She sat beside me on the bench and fumbled through her books and binders.

I chuckled. "You know, we are in the twenty-first century. Don't you have digital books?"

She looked at me and smiled, a genuinely adorable smile. "I like paper. I mean, don't get me wrong. I have a lot of stuff on my notepad, but there are just some things that are better on real paper." She found what she was looking for. "Oh, and here we are. You need help with history."

"That's right."

"What do you want to start with?"

"You're the pro. You tell me."

"Well, I should probably see about getting you started on your English assignment."

"And what is that?"

"We have a three-thousand-word essay that we have to write on a subject."

"What subject?"

She pulled out a sheet of paper and handed it to me. "Here's a list of options. You might want to choose something else entirely... if you have a really good idea. However, I suggest that you take one of these."

Born Rotten
(A Married in Malibu Novella)

I looked at the list. "These are some damned dull subjects. Who the hell can write three thousand words about composting, or ants or clouds? Damn… there's even the life of the hummingbird."

She looked at me. "Well, I'm sure that if you go through the entire list, you'll find something that you're interested in. Although, truth be told, your own personal interest in the subject is beside the point. The point of this essay is to show your ability to effectively articulate facts and opinions on any subject."

"Surnames," I muttered. "What's that?"

"Halliwell," she said.

I looked up at her. "Yeah?"

Again with that adorable smile. "That's a surname. Halliwell. Chen. Rhee. Smith."

"Oh. You mean last names."

"That's right."

"Stupid subject."

"I don't know. It could be interesting. You know… you could find out the origin of names, the meaning of names, the most unusual names. There's a bunch of stuff."

I shrugged.

She pulled out her electronic device and started to look up stuff. "Here," she said as she tilted the notepad to me. "Look at this. Halliwell. Do you even know what your own name means?

"Never really thought about it."

"Comes from Old English with many spellings… essentially 'holy' and 'well' or 'spring'… like water well or spring water." She looked at me all excited. "Isn't that cool?"

I pressed a doubting grin.

"Anyway, here's more. You can start with this."

I leaned closer to her to look at the screen; the history of surnames. But all I could really think about was the sweet smell of her hair, her skin, her breath.

Born Rotten
(A Married in Malibu Novella)

Damn.

Not only had I gotten the genius girl of the school to help me out, but I had gotten the sweetest thing I'd ever come across.

"Do you have a notebook?" she said.

"You mean an electronic thing like yours? No. I got nothing."

"You *have* nothing," she said.

"That's what I said. I got nothing."

She shook her head. "You don't *got* nothing. You *have* nothing."

I leaned back. "Ah, hell. Don't get me started on that stuff."

"What stuff?" she said, looking at me with a bit of a prissy expression on her sweet face. "Grammar?"

"Fine. Fine," I said through an exasperated grunt. "I don't *have* a notebook."

"Well then," she said as she pulled a spiral notebook out of her bag. "You can have one of mine."

I took the notebook and looked at it, flipped it open to see all the blank pages, then looked up at her. "Okay. Now what?"

"Now you take down notes, silly." She handed me her notepad. "Here. Take a look and jot down a few ideas."

For the next fifteen minutes, I took notes on the various usage of surnames around the world. All the while, Taylor sat patiently beside me, giving me pointers every now and again.

"I think you're off to a good start," she said. "All you have to do now is take those notes and turn them into an essay. Tomorrow, you can take down more notes. Before you know it, you'll have three thousand words down."

The next day, however, we touched on math. She might as well have been talking another language.

Born Rotten
(A Married in Malibu Novella)

"What the hell am I ever going to use this for?" I said. "I mean, I know how to add and subtract and multiply and divide. Oh, and I even know a bit about fractions and percentages. But this…? No one uses math like this."

"People do use it," she said. "It all depends on what you want to do when you get out of school."

"Well, I can tell you that I'm going to be doing something that does not involve any of this shit."

She glared at me.

"What?"

"Do you really have to swear all the time? Don't get me wrong. I'm not a prude or anything. I can understand the occasional need to use a good f-bomb."

I chuckled. "You can't even say it, can you?"

"What do you mean?"

"The f-word. Say it."

"No."

"Come on. It won't hurt you."

"If the occasion doesn't call for it, I won't use it."

I looked pointedly at her. "You used it the other day in the principal's office."

She cocked a brow. "Well now, you see. That occasion called for it. You were getting on my nerves."

"And now?"

"Now you're just being annoying and childish."

I let out a loud laugh. "Childish. Ha. I'll have you know that I am eighteen years old."

"Then I suggest you start acting like it." She poked me in the ribs, causing me to jump back with an unexpected laugh.

"Stop it," I muttered.

She poked me again.

"Stop it!"

She poked me once more.

Born Rotten
(A Married in Malibu Novella)

"That does it." I turned on her, tickling her until she fell off the bench and we were both on the grass.

"Okay!" she shouted. "I give up. I cry uncle. I surrender."

Straddling her, I suddenly became acutely aware of the heat emanating from her body and how hard my dick had become. My brain told me to get off her, but my body had other ideas. I grabbed her wrists and pinned her to the ground.

Our heavy breathing was the only sound and as our eyes met, all giggling and laughing faded. Was she feeling what I felt?

Damn. What was I feeling? Curious? Intrigue? Definitely aroused. But by brainiac?

No, I couldn't. I shouldn't.

I got off her and offered her a helping hand to get her on her feet.

"Well," she said in all seriousness. "Now that playtime is over, let's get down to business. We'll set aside math for now."

"Good."

She reached out for the notebook that she'd given me the day before. Before I could stop her, she opened it.

"Let's see where you are with your essay."

"Wait!" I shouted. "Give it back."

"Why? I'm going to have to read it if I'm to assess your writing abilities."

She turned the page and frowned.

"Don't read that," I said as she stood and stepped back.

"What is this?"

"Just some stuff I jotted down."

"Is this a poem?"

"No. Never mind. Let's get back to the math problems."

Born Rotten
(A Married in Malibu Novella)

"In my dreams, it's never true. I always run back to you. The sun is bright, you're at my side. The nights are long, I know I'm wrong."

"Please," I said softly. "Give it back."

She looked at me. "This is nice. I don't know what sort of stanza you're using, but…"

"Look," I said as I tried to reach for the notebook. "It's just words…"

She kept the book out of my grasp. "Tell me more."

Her lips moved as she continued to read. "Oh, my God," she said. "It's a song, right?" She looked up at me with that angelic smile. "It's a song. Oh, right."

"Not yet… it's just a few ideas."

"Let's see… *In… my… dreams, it's never true,*" she sang. "*I always run back… to… you.*"

Shit. She even sang like an angel.

"I love it," she said. Then she shoved the notebook into my hand. "I obviously don't know the melody that you have in mind. Sing it for me."

I shook my head. I honestly couldn't remember the last time that I felt so embarrassed. "I'm not ready yet."

As the next few days passed, we concentrated on math, and she didn't bring up the song again. For some strange reason, I was disappointed. I guess a part of me really did want her to know all about the music that I had inside me.

I wrote more songs, writing my heart out, but she never looked at my notebook. Only two weeks later, when she asked to see my essay, did she finally get a glimpse of some of the other songs that I'd scribbled down in the same notebook.

"More songs, huh?" she said, a little disinterested as she flipped through the pages then returned to the essay.

"It helps me to write out how I feel."

"I can understand that."

Born Rotten
(A Married in Malibu Novella)

She was silent as she read the three pages of my essay. With a red pen in hand, she circled something. "Here you wrote, 'It had tooken them a year...'. 'Tooken' isn't a word."

I grimaced and sought the right word. "It had *took* them?"

She shook her head. "It had *taken* them..."

She finished reading the rest then flipped a few pages more until she once again came to my latest song.

"You can read it if you like," I muttered softly.

She glanced at me then looked back at the page and read aloud: "What can you do when the pain never leaves. How can a heart mend when all it wants is to grieve? Like a punch in the gut, you groan and move on. Like a meal all alone, its tasteless and bland." She stared at the page for a long time, her eyes becoming glassy with unshed tears. "I do hope that one day you'll let me hear you sing these songs."

I shrugged. "Maybe."

"There's a depth of emotion that is quite… touching. What makes you write such dark and sad lyrics?"

I took the book from her, sighed and leaned back against the bench. While I was willing to allow her to read a few words here and there, I wasn't yet ready to open up to her. "It's none of your business."

"I see." She was silent as she drummed the fingers of one hand over the back of the other. "I long to fly high as an eagle."

Creasing my brow, I shot her a curious glance.

"My heart crests as I soar ever higher. I'm free to do just as I care. I dive. I dart. I soar. I flutter. Atop a pine I perch, reigning over the forest that is my realm. Atop a pine, I'm at peace, for I do as I dare."

Born Rotten
(A Married in Malibu Novella)

"Is that a song?" I said.

She shook her head. "I don't know much about music. It's poetry… just words."

"It's nice."

"Thanks."

"It sounds kind of sad," I said. "Why?"

"None of your business," she said as she turned and looked at me with a teasing grin.

I smiled back at her, my first real and genuine smile since meeting her. My gut flipped upside down and the palms of my hands grew clammy. She had a way of digging deep inside me and making me see things about myself that I had never seen before.

Chapter 5

<u>Dex</u>

After a week I decided it was time to go back to my aunt's house in Santa Ana and grab some of my stuff. As I arrived at her house, part of me hoped to see her up and about so that I could say goodbye. Then again, things would be simpler if she was passed out and I could just sneak in and sneak out without fuss.

I opened the door and was instantly assailed by the scent of cat pee. Damn. I'd already forgotten what her place smelled like.

I tiptoed in. But then I realized that there was no need to be so careful. As usual, she was face down on the couch.

"Thanks for all you've done all the same," I muttered as I went to the plastic drawers she'd bought for me at the discount store. All my worldly possessions were in those two little drawers.

I grabbed everything and shoved it all into a grocery bag then headed back out to the car.

"Well, well," a sleazy voice said as I put the bag in the trunk. "Look what the cat dragged back to Santa Ana."

I turned to face Hector. "This isn't your turf. What you want?"

He shot a glance at Alex who stood beside him. "Tell him, Al."

"We've expanded," Alex said as he looked down at the sidewalk.

I had pulled my car as far into my aunt's driveway as I could, but the back bumper was over the sidewalk, as were my feet.

"You're now standing six inches within our territory."

"Not for long," I said as I slammed the trunk shut. "I'm out of here. You won't ever have to see this mug again."

I turned to head to the driver side door, but Alex grabbed me and pushed me up against the car. Before I knew it, I was punched in the gut, then clipped on the ear before getting a swift and teeth shattering upper cut to the chin.

I muttered something incoherent as I tried to remain upright.

"Are you trying to call your dear old auntie, Dex?" Hector chanted. "Is she going to come out and save you?"

Laughing, Alex threw another punch and another and another. I was on the verge of blacking out and I knew that if I did, they'd kill me. They would keep hitting and kicking until I'd breathed my last breath.

"What's going on over there?"

Alex shot a sidelong glance at the neighbor who'd just arrived with her two kids.

Born Rotten
(A Married in Malibu Novella)

"What are you boys doing over there?"

"Mind your fucking business," Hector shouted. But he nonetheless gave me a last and long hard glare, spit on me and walked away with Alex close behind him.

With them gone, the neighbor went into her house and left me there to figure things out on my own. No doubt she wasn't aware just how badly I was hurt.

But shit. I was hurting.

I looked up at my aunt's house and considered my options. I could try to wake her up and get her to bring me to the hospital.

Hell no. There was no point in trying.

Leaning heavily into my car, I stumbled to the driver side door, opened it, and slid in.

Option two; I could drive myself to the hospital.

But as I tried to look at myself in the rearview mirror to assess just how hurt I was, I realized that my eyes were nearly swollen shut. I could barely make out my own face and I knew that it was only going to get worse.

Taylor, I thought. Would she come? Would she care? Would she just think me so fucking hopeless and helpless?

I pulled out my phone. I was soon going to find out.

"Hello?" Taylor said as she answered.

"Taylor?" I mumbled with difficulty. My swollen and cut lips made it difficult to talk.

"Dex?"

"I'm in Santa Ana," I managed to say.

"What happened?"

"The gang got me. They got me bad."

"Shit. You're in luck. I'm just outside of Santa Ana. I'll be right over. Where are you exactly?"

I gave her the address and hung up. For the next five minutes, I went in and out of consciousness.

Born Rotten
(A Married in Malibu Novella)

"Dex?" Taylor whispered as she opened the car door. "Oh, my God."

I tried to look at her. I was barely able to open one eye and not at all the other.

"We have to get you to the hospital," she said. "Come on. Get into my car."

She helped me out and settled me into her car. For a small and slight girl, she sure had a whole lot of arm power. I have no idea how she managed to get me to her car.

But five minutes later, we were pulling up to the emergency entrance to the hospital. After only a few minutes in triage, I was called on and went in to see the doctor.

"I'll wait out here," Taylor said.

They did a decent job of patching me up and making sure that I had no serious injuries, but they wanted to keep me overnight all the same.

Just as I was about to drift off to sleep, an angel walked into the room.

"Hey there," her sweet voice said.

I cracked open my decent eye. "You're still here," I said, a little groggy from the painkiller they'd given me.

"Of course, I'm still here." She smiled. "I wanted to make sure that everything was all right before I left."

"They're keeping me overnight."

"So I see."

She set her hand over mine and I'd never felt such a strong bond with anyone. For the first time in my life, I felt that I had someone to count on, someone to lean on. Someone who cared.

"I'll be back tomorrow morning to pick you up." She patted my hand. "Get some rest."

Chapter 6

<u>Dex</u>

The next morning, she was there when I opened my eyes. I got the okay from the doctor to leave, but I had no idea where I was going.

Taylor wheeled me out of the room, into the elevator and down to the entrance. Once outside, I got on my own two feet, and we walked to her car.

"I'm sorry to have to put you through all this," I said as I got into the passenger seat and looked up at her as she prepared to close the car door behind me.

"No worries," she said, all chipper and cheery. "It's all good."

"I hate to ask you for another favor," I said, realizing just how needy I was being.

"Sure. Shoot."

"I came down to get my stuff from my aunt's."

"Okay…"

"My stuff is still in the trunk of my car. Come to think of it, maybe you should drop me off there and I'll drive back to Irvine."

"Don't be ridiculous," she said as she took off toward my aunt's house. "You can't drive in your condition. You probably can't even see the road in front of you."

She was right there. Everything was a blur… except her.

We arrived at my aunt's house and Taylor held out her hand. I looked at her and shrugged.

"The keys to your car," she said.

"Oh." I frowned, trying to remember where I'd left them. Then I shook my head. "They're probably in the car."

"Okay." She got out, found the keys in the front passenger seat, opened the trunk and brought my stuff into her car. Getting back into the driver's seat, she looked at me. "All set?"

"All set." I leaned back against the headrest as she drove off. I couldn't believe how comfortable and secure I felt with her.

I was barely aware of the drive to Irvine. Only when she stopped and killed the engine did I open my eyes. She'd pulled up in front of the church.

Damn it. Did she know that I was staying there… in the parking lot… in my car… the car that I no longer had?

Pressing her lips together as if regretting what she was about to say, she looked at me. "I thought you might be more comfortable staying here."

I looked at the church. "What do you mean, *here*?"

"Off to that side there are living quarters. You'd have them all to yourself."

"Oh?"

Darn. She knew that I was homeless.

"It's nothing lavish. Nothing fancy. But it's comfortable and clean."

Unsure, I shrugged.

"It's where the minister typically lives."

"And where is he living now?"

"When his family grew, he decided to move to a house… one with more than just one bedroom."

I looked at her. "And how is it that you know so much about this minister?"

She smiled. "He's my father."

I heard myself gulp loudly then noticed her amused grin.

"Don't worry," she said. "He's not the brimstone and fire type of minister."

I looked at the church, still not sure.

"It's either that, or I take you home with me and you'll meet my parents… minister and all."

Smiling, I nodded. "I'll take the church."

Born Rotten
(A Married in Malibu Novella)

"That's what I thought." She opened the car door and got out. "Come on. I'll help get you settled."

Getting me settled consisted of her helping me into the apartment and getting me to the comfy sofa that sat right smack in the middle of the tiny living room. She then headed out to get my bags of stuff and put everything away in the closet and dresser drawers.

"So," she said as she sat on the edge of the sofa. "What do you think?"

"Reminds me of a grandma's place."

She laughed. "Yeah. It is kind of old fashioned and stuffy. But... the fridge works, the stove works, the plumbing works and... well... what more could you ask for?"

"It's perfect," I said, regretting my negative take on the place. "Really, it is."

She clapped her hands to her knees and got back up. "You must be starving. How about I fix you something to eat. How does a nice ham sandwich sound?"

"Great."

I sat up a bit and flicked on the television. Cartoons.

"What day are we?" I said when she brought me my sandwich.

"Saturday."

I looked up at her. "Oh. That explains how you're here with me instead of in class."

"Speaking of which…"

As I bit into the sandwich, she opened my bag and pulled out my notebook. The big musical note that I'd drawn on the cover probably tipped her off.

"More songs?"

Before I could answer, she opened it and read;

What's the matter, Mother?
Is my face too dirty for you?
What's the deal, Father?

Born Rotten
(A Married in Malibu Novella)

I'm not good enough to make the team?
I'm your disappointment.
I'm your failure.
I'm the embarrassment in front of the neighbors.
I sing too loud.
I curse too much
Why the hell do I bother trying?
I'm just not good enough.

"Wow, Dex," she whispered. "This is…damn. It's just so…"

With tears in her eyes, she leaned in and kissed my forehead, as if seeking to kiss away all the pain.

She almost did.

"When am I going to hear the music that goes with this?"

"Someday."

"Okay," she said. "I can be patient. But…"

"But what?"

"If you're feeling up to it, I have a little surprise for you tomorrow."

I was definitely intrigued. And the next morning when she arrived, all dressed up in a pretty pale blue dress, I was even more intrigued.

"Where are you bringing me?" I said.

"Are you up for it?"

"Depends on what *it* is."

"All I ask is that you come downstairs to the main building."

"You mean, the church."

She nodded.

I wasn't into religion. I didn't see the point.

"Please," she said. "I promise you won't be disappointed."

"Give me a minute to get dressed."

Minutes later I was following her down to the church that was packed.

"Wow. I didn't think so many people went to church."

Born Rotten
(A Married in Malibu Novella)

"My father is a very well-liked minister," she said. "Here," she said as she gestured to a vacant place. "Sit here."

"Where are you going?"

"Just sit here," she whispered. "I'll meet up with you later."

As I sat down, she took the side aisle and discreetly made her way up to the front of the church then disappeared.

After an inspiring sermon by the minister, an older woman at the front of the church began playing the organ. Behind her, a dozen women, all decked out in long red robes, came out and lined up in two rows. In the center front row was Taylor.

I was mesmerized. What was she doing there?

I soon found out.

The dozen women began to sing to the music of the organ. It was sweet and heavenly... like nothing I'd ever heard before.

But then my heart was captured for good. Taylor stepped forward and sang a portion of the song all on her own. While I'd heard her play around and sing a vague melody to my lyrics, this… this was completely different. It was clearly a song that she knew, a song that she felt. A song that she believed. And she sang it with all her heart.

And my heart wanted to sing with her.

At that moment, I knew I wanted to sing like her…with all my heart, every feeling, every emotion, every ups and downs that I've ever felt.

She had touched a chord deep within me that had never been touched before. No one had ever cared more about me than she did. Not even I had cared about me as much. Without even knowing who I was, she had already challenged me to change my rotten ways and believe in something better from the first time she met me.

She truly was someone special.

I wondered if she knew just how important she'd become in my life. I wondered if she knew that she was now more than a friend… more than family. That my heart ached when I thought of her. That my heart pounded faster when I'm with her.

How could she know what I, myself, was just now realizing? That I was falling in love with her.

Chapter 7

<u>Taylor</u>

I was a good girl. I'd always been. I wasn't interested in going out to drink and party and go wild.

No. All that mattered to me was that I maintained my straight A's. All that mattered was that I remain a good student… the best student… the so-called model student.

Yeah. I modeled everything… studious, long hours, conscientious. I was kind and polite to everyone I met, even when they didn't deserve it. I was charitable and generous… after all, I was the pastor's daughter.

I had to be good, right?

Born Rotten
(A Married in Malibu Novella)

But from the very moment that I set eyes on Dex Halliwell, it seemed that keeping up with that good girl reputation was a constant battle.

My body suddenly longed to be bad. My body was having some very non-good-girl reactions to him, and I didn't know what to do about it.

Dex. Dark, brooding, mysterious, enigmatic Dex. Sexy, appealing, magnetic Dex. Everything my body seemed to crave.

And everything that I knew my parents would loath.

As I sat on the front stoop of the church waiting for him to arrive for his tutoring session, I thought back to just how intimidated I'd really been when we'd first met. He was like no one I'd ever come across before.

"We're not meant to be together," I muttered to myself under the rustling of the leaves high up in the trees.

Then why does he get under my skin the way that he does? Why does he only need to smile, and I melt? Why is that low, smoldering voice able to reach so deep inside me?

Why? Why? Why?

The notion of sensuality was new to me. Sex was new to me… and the way that I felt when he would sometimes look at me was new to me.

On the other side of the intersection, I saw him coming my way. He wore a tattered leather hat low over his brow and he'd recently begun to allow the hint of a shadow to cover his jaw. Wearing a simple black button-down shirt that had a few too many buttons that were left unfastened, he was effortlessly sexy.

With that confident and easy stride, he came up to me and held out a sheet of paper.

"What's this?" I said as I reached out to take the sheet.

"That, my dear Tay, is a B minus," he said, beaming. "Thanks to you."

Born Rotten
(A Married in Malibu Novella)

He sat beside me and stretched his jean clad legs out in front of him as he set his elbows down on the top step and leaned back.

Again, that effortless sexuality.

"Wow, a B minus," I said, staring at the big red grade marked in the corner. "And in math no less." I looked at him. "You must be very proud."

"And you should be proud, too," he said. "After all, this is all because of you."

I chuckled. "I think you had a bit to do with it, too."

It's nice to see you smiling, I wanted to say. His smile, as slight and almost shy as it was, lit up his face. I'd grown so accustomed to the constant brooding that it was almost like looking at a completely different person when he smiled.

"I have to admit," I said. "It's a whole lot better than I thought you'd get."

"You and me, both," he said with a snort. "Hell, I would have been happy with a C. Who knows. Maybe one day I'll be getting A's like you."

"I don't see why you couldn't."

His smile broadened and I saw something in his eyes that I had never really seen before; hope and optimism.

It was a surprising glimpse into the boy that he really was. He was broken and he fought hard to make himself look like he had it all together, that everything was under control. Truth was his life was far from under control.

But this was the first step to taking back that control.

"Well," Dex said. "I finally gave in that essay that I had to write for English class, so… we'll see how that turns out. Maybe I'll even get my first A."

"I think that you're a lot smarter than you think you are."

Born Rotten
(A Married in Malibu Novella)

"You mean than I was led to believe that I was."

"Really?" I said. "Who told you that you weren't smart?"

He snorted. "Heh... everybody. My aunt, the teachers, the principals, other kids. I was just a dumbass." He glanced up at me. "So why bother trying, heh?"

"Well, I'm happy to see that you're trying now."

He sat up and looked at me. "Why should you care one way or another?"

Why, indeed.

I shrugged. "I just think that it's such a waste to see a student slip through the cracks. It's a catastrophe as far as I'm concerned. I mean, look at all the opportunities that are going to be open to you now that you're getting your grades up."

Once again, he leaned back onto his elbows. "All I want to do is get through high school. After that, I'm going to be making music."

A wistful smile crossed his face. He was so far removed from the arrogant bully that he'd portrayed himself to be on that first day… the bully who'd simply regarded me as just a plain Jane nerd.

"You've been promising to let me hear your music for a while now," I said. "How about we celebrate this B minus of yours with a song?"

"Ha," he let out. "Nice try. I'm not ready."

"What are you afraid of?" I said, my tone a clear challenge.

"I'm not afraid."

"Yes, you are. You're afraid that I won't like it."

"Why should your opinion matter one way or another?" he said, his wall of arrogance coming up. "It's not like you're a musician or something."

"Exactly," I said. "Why should my opinion matter? Therefore, why should you be afraid to let me hear one song… just one?"

He sat up, glared at me, then stood. "Fine. Come on inside."

His steps were almost angry as he stomped his way to the small apartment adjacent to the church. Once inside, he pointed to the sofa. "Sit."

I dutifully sat down as he reached for his acoustic guitar and tossed the strapped over his shoulder. He strummed a chord, adjusted a string or two, then strummed again. Satisfied with the tuning, he looked at me.

For a second, I thought he was going to back out. There was something innocent and unsure in his eyes… like he was about to unveil something big and personal.

Then his fingers began to pick at the strings, an odd and melancholy melody that was both haunting and inspiring.

"It's dark when I get up," he sang. *"The sun won't rise. It's hard to bring it up. You're on my mind. What kind of world am I looking at? It's not my choice but I do think that… I'm on my own. I'm on my own."*

Except for one quick glance up at me, he kept his head down as he looked at his fingers on the strings.

"People come and go. No one ever cares. The only thing I know, is you're never there. It makes no sense and I wonder why. I look at them as I hurry by. I'm on my own. I'm on my own."

He stopped suddenly and set the guitar down.

"Why'd you stop?" I said. "That was good. That was nice."

"That was enough," he said bluntly.

"You have a very good voice," I said.

He shrugged. "I'm no Steve Perry or anything."

"Well," I admitted. "I didn't hear enough to make more of an assessment than that, but you…

Born Rotten
(A Married in Malibu Novella)

You emote. You draw the listener in. You make me want to know more… to hear more."

Chewing on the inside of his cheek, he nodded.

On a lark, I reached out for his guitar and settled it on my lap.

He frowned and looked at me skeptically but said nothing.

I began to strum the few basic chords that I knew. *"I've been 'round the world, you know,"* I sang. *"Come back home to my favorite folks. It's a happy time just hanging out. Wondering what you're all about."*

Glancing at him, I continued to strum the happy and uplifting chords to my happy and uplifting song. But his eyes remained steadfastly on my hands, not my face.

"If you laugh at me, what does it say about you? Cause I can laugh at myself, and what does that do? Take your weapons away, and what do you

have? You have to look at yourself and figure it out. Cause I'm happy... no matter what. Cause I'm happy... even if you're not."

Sensing his disinterest, I stopped and bit the corner of my lip. "I guess my music isn't as introspective as yours is. I mean, I still have to work on the lyrics a bit, but..."

He remained silent as he took back his guitar. I pursed my lips, regretting sharing my song with him.

"Try again," he said as he began to pick the chords that I'd clumsily played.

Somehow, my simple chords sounded like heaven under his touch. They were more melodic and uplifting.

I sang the first verse again, marveling at how different the song sounded. When we reached the chorus he stopped.

"Where were you going with the chorus?" he said.

Born Rotten
(A Married in Malibu Novella)

"Go to G, then C, then A and E, and back to G."

He nodded and continued to play as I sang the chorus. Tears welled up as I sang. My little song was a simple little ditty, something I'd written just for fun. But he had turned it into something that sounded great.

"How do you do that?" I said when we ended the song.

"Picking?" He shrugged. "Practice, I guess."

"Your song sounded so... I don't know... dark and moody... almost sad."

"Minor chords tend to have that effect. Then again, I'm quite fond of the Phrygian mode. Also Aeolian can make just about anything sound sad. It's the flat 6 that gives it that real melancholy sense of longing."

"What's that? Aeolian? And Phrygian?" I said, showing my limited knowledge of music.

He shrugged again. It was a move I'd seen him do many times, often when I was complimenting him, as if he couldn't take the compliment.

"It's just a series of chords that play well with the mood I'm in. Locrian sometimes suits me, too. Of course Mixolydian is a pretty common mode in rock but…"

"Can you play me a happy song?" I said, hoping to challenge him.

He smirked, then looked sidelong at me. "I don't think so."

"Why not?"

"I don't do 'happy'."

"Why not?"

He sat back into the corner of the sofa and idly strummed the guitar strings. "I guess I'm just not the 'happy' sort of guy."

"Is that by choice?"

He looked up at me from under his dark brow then tilted his head back and ran his thumb and index finger over the corners of his mouth. "Choice," he said softly. "What is a choice? Did I choose to have my father run out of my life? Did I choose to have my drug addicted mother die on me? Did I choose to then move in with her sister, my alcoholic aunt? Did I choose to get beaten up by the neighborhood gang? Did I choose to have failing grades because I couldn't keep up? Did I choose to have such a rotten life?"

I was silent for a long moment as I thought of all he'd been through. It just seemed so unfair.

His jaw slack as he suck on his bottom lip, he looked down at his lap.

"You chose to come here to Irvine," I finally said. "I think that so far, that's proving to be a good choice. You chose to accept to be tutored by me, even though I'm not the type of girl you would usually prefer to hang out with, but… if I do say so myself, I think it's been a good thing. And you've finally shared your music with me. Those are all choices that you made."

The corner of his mouth curved up slightly. "You're right," he said in that slow, almost arrogant way he had at times. "You're not the type of girl I usually prefer to hang out with."

Ouch.

"But I wish I had."

Oh?

"Maybe if I'd hung out with girls like you a little more often, I wouldn't be struggling to get my life together right now."

"The important thing is that you're getting your life together now. There's no point wondering what could have been. Look straight ahead of you and look at what's to be."

He chuckled.

"Do you always have such an annoyingly optimistic view on life?"

I laughed. "Pretty much."

Born Rotten
(A Married in Malibu Novella)

He leaned back and looked at me with a crooked smile. There was also a barely perceptible nod… a nod of acceptance.

Perhaps I was finally getting through to him. Perhaps he wasn't so rotten after all.

Chapter 8

<u>Taylor</u>

Only a week after that B minus, Dex arrived at our tutoring session with another beaming smile.

"Does that smile mean that you got another good grade?" I said.

"My essay," he said, holding it up. "I got a B."

"Dex, that's great."

"Not only that but I got a B plus."

I jumped up to hug him. For a fractured moment, I wondered what had gotten into me as I anticipated him pushing me off him, but then he reciprocated, pulling me tightly into his arms.

"I never thought that getting good grades could feel so good," he said as he pulled back and looked down at me. "And it's all because of you."

Born Rotten
(A Married in Malibu Novella)

We stared at one another for a strangely electric moment. His arms around me, his face so close… so close….

Then he leaned in and kissed me. His lips were warm and soft against mine as I had imagined it would be. I floated on a cloud. It was beautiful, sensual, passionate all while being so sweet.

"I have a new song that I want you to hear," he said as he pulled away from the kiss, grabbed my hand and led me to his apartment. He threw his school stuff down on the counter and reached for his guitar.

I was thrilled to see him so eager to share a song with me. Since the last time he'd picked up the guitar, he hadn't shared anything.

He strummed the guitar all while keeping rhythm by slapping the body of the guitar with his hand. The rhythm was fast, feisty… almost festive.

"Bring me the girl that I want to know," he sang. *"Tell me where she is, and to her I will go.*

Turn me upside down with an innocent smile. Don't care if it rains, I will sing all the while."

He smiled and looked at me. I had never seen him look so happy.

"Is this what they meant, you can open your heart," he went on. *"Is this how it feels, aching when we're apart. Time drags on when you're not around. Only for you, I'll play the clown."*

I laughed. It was a funny, sentimental and somewhat quirky song. And at the same time, my heart soared. Was the song meant for me? Was I the girl that he would go to?

When the song ended, I clapped enthusiastically. "I knew you had it in you," I said. "You really are capable of writing a happy song."

He offered me a smirk. "Not so fast," he said. "There's a final verse where the girl dies in a car accident."

I frowned. "What a horrible thing to say… or to sing."

He gave me a slow-motion playful punch in the arm. "I'm just pulling your leg. The girl doesn't die."

Laughing, I gave him a playful push, but instead of backing away, he pulled me into his arms.

"I'm not really sure I like what you're doing to me," he said, his voice a lusty growl. "You make me feel things… things that I think will eventually hurt."

I smiled at him. "Funny. I was just thinking the same thing. You make me feel things that I never even knew existed. You have my body reacting in ways that… well… in ways that I never thought I would. In ways that I thought only other girls… those really pretty girls got to feel."

He tilted his head to the side and furrowed his brow. "Those really pretty girls?"

"Yeah. You know. Those girls with pretty clothes, with sexy shoes and with fashion sense.

Those girls who know how to do their hair… who wear make-up.”

With his hands down around my waist, he pulled me tightly to him, tight enough that our pelvises collided. “Those girls don’t have what you have.”

“Yeah. Yeah,” I droned on with a sigh. “I know the story. Those girls don’t have brains. I’m smart. That’s worth something. That’s worth a lot more than being pretty.”

He shook his head. “That’s not what I meant. I meant that you’re a lot prettier than those other girls.”

“Aha!” I let out. “Nice try.”

Leaning in until his forehead butted up against mine, he whispered, “I’m serious. Those girls might be flashy and look good from afar, but you’re the real deal. You have a face like one of those really pretty and expensive dolls… you know… the ones that are made out of… Well, I don't know what they're made of, but they're real pretty."

"Porcelain," I said. "They're porcelain dolls."

He ran his fingers over my cheek, down the side of my neck and around to the nape of my neck. "That's what you are, a brilliant yet delicate porcelain doll. My porcelain doll."

He pulled me in for a kiss that devoured me, and I willingly gave myself to him. Tender and patient, he took off my shirt.

I shivered, not from the sudden coolness to my skin, but from the very thought of being nude before him, even though I still had my bra and jeans on.

Kissing my shoulder and down my collar bone, he reached around to unclasp my bra and slipped it off. He looked down at my breasts as he bit his bottom lip. "You're so beautiful, it hurts."

His eyes devoured me, and I felt more beautiful than I've ever felt before.

"Have you ever been touched before?" he said.

I shook my head.

"Do you want to be touched?"

Inhaling deeply, I looked at him. I hadn't expected the question and I didn't know what to say. Of course, my body longed for his touch, but my upbringing told me to say 'no'. If I allowed him to touch me... that way... where would it lead?

"How about we take it slow?" he whispered.

I nodded.

He gently set his open hand over my breast then closed his hand, pinching my nipple between his thumb and index finger in the process.

I immediately shuddered and a surprisingly husky rasp escaped my lips.

"You like that, huh?"

His other hand rose to do the same to my other breast. My knees weakened and I suddenly felt the need to sit down.

But before I could, Dex released my breasts and rid me of my sandals and jeans. Standing there in my underwear, I looked at him. He was still fully dressed.

"Would you feel more comfortable if I took off a bit of my clothes, too?"

I nodded and he proceeded to slowly remove one article of clothing after another until he, too, stood in his underwear.

My body tingled with anticipation. Were we really doing this? Were we really going to go through with this?

I'm a good girl, my angelic conscience screamed out.

Sex before marriage, my mother's voice called out. How could you?

But there I was, in his arms, enjoying the sweet little kisses that he set all over my skin.

He guided me back until I was sitting, then lying on the sofa. "I want you, Taylor. I want you so bad."

Take me, I wanted to shout.

Oh, my God. Who are you? Who is this sex fiend who is ready to let everything that has ever been good about her fly out the door?

I'm just a girl, I answered my questioning conscience. *I'm just a girl who wants to enjoy being with the boy she likes.*

And I do like him.

He finally took off my underwear, then rid himself of his.

I'd never seen a penis before... not in real life... other than my little nephew when he was a baby and I'd watched my cousin as she'd changed his diaper.

"Are you sure?" he said, looking straight into my eyes.

Born Rotten
(A Married in Malibu Novella)

"Have you done this before?" The question came out before I'd even thought of it, and I wasn't sure I wanted to hear the answer.

But he simply smiled as he came to lie over me. He lowered his head to kiss my nipple, sending ripples of pleasure throughout my body. I couldn't help moaning.

"You're so beautiful, Tay," Dex said. "From the first time I saw you, I thought you were exquisite." Then he slowly nudge his way inside me. Tightening my jaw, I tensed up as I awaited the pain that should accompany his penetration, but other than a brief moment of discomfort, I felt nothing… except the joy of having him.

So, this is what it's like, I thought.

I joined in the rhythm of his motions, rocking my hips in this strange new dance. While I sighed with the pleasure of it all, a part of me wanted to laugh; laugh at the girl I'd always been; laugh at the prudish notions I'd had. I'd always been so intent on being the model student, the model daughter, the model person… never had I imagined that I could possibly be so reckless and wild.

As Dex continued to make sweet and tender love to me, I looked into his eyes and marveled at the transformation he'd brought about in me.

I was in heaven and never wanted to leave his arms.

Chapter 9

<u>Taylor</u>

It was our little secret. My mother and father had no idea that I had a boy living in the apartment by the church. Nor did they know that I was dating him… officially dating him.

No one knew except us.

We'd gotten into the habit of hanging out in a large room, something akin to a rec room, that was specifically created and furnished for tweens and teens.

"How come no one ever comes here?" Dex said as he settled into one of the many bean bag chairs strewn around the large room.

I shrugged. "My father's congregation is a bit older," I said. "I think the average age is just over sixty. Not many of them have any kids young enough to come here."

"All the better for us," he said.

Nodding, I nudged the neighboring bean bag chair closer to him, then plopped down in it, throwing my head into Dex's lap.

"So," he said as he ran his fingers through my hair. "What's this surprise that you wanted to tell me about?"

I smiled up at him. "You know how you're always telling me that my poetry is special."

He nodded.

"Well, I decided to enter a poem into a local poetry contest."

"Seriously?" he said, a broad grin on his face. "Tay, that's great. It's about time others get the chance to appreciate the talent that you are. You have such a way with words… so deep and thoughtful… so lyrical. I have no doubt you'll win."

"If I win at the local level, I could win $250. I'll then go on to the state's competition where I could win $1000."

"That sure would be cool," he said.

I shrugged. "Yeah, but I hear that competition is tough. There are a lot of great poets out there."

"Hey, where are all the optimistic and encouraging words you're always throwing at me? You know, like how you're always telling me that I'm talented, and that I should share my music with others? How come you don't use that same optimism on yourself?"

I shrugged again. It was easier to be optimistic and confident for him than for myself.

He ran the back of his finger down my cheek. "No one writes like you, Tay. I mean there might be some poets out there who have nice rhymes, interesting stanzas and pretty floral prose, but you… the depth and emotion… it can't be beat."

"Thanks for believing in me."

He cupped my face in his hands. "I think it's time you practiced what you preach, little girl. Now, let me hear you be positive. You're going to win, aren't you?"

I looked into his tender eyes.

"Aren't you?" he insisted.

I smiled and he cracked up laughing.

"I guess," I said.

"Aren't you?"

"Okay. Okay. I'm going to win."

"That's my girl," he said, his eyes beaming with such love and admiration for me.

My stomach turned upside down, much the way it always did when he looked at me that way.

Born Rotten
(A Married in Malibu Novella)

"You know, I was beginning to wonder if I should trust you at all."

"What do you mean?" I said.

"Well, for all the times that you've told me to believe in myself, and here you are now not believing in yourself… well, how do you think that looks? You look unreliable, like you don't believe in your own words."

"Okay," I said. "You've made your point. I will never, ever doubt myself again."

He leaned in to kiss me. His lips were so soft and warm, and it didn't take long for me to forget all about poetry.

"I got my math grade back," he said as he abruptly pulled away from the kiss.

Still in the fog of that kiss, I just looked at him.

"I passed," he said.

"Oh," I said, finally shaking off the effects of the kiss. "That's good. I'm so proud of you."

And, on that optimistic note, we pulled apart and took out our notebooks. His essay was really coming along great, even though he was spending a little too much time writing songs rather than his essay.

Chapter 10

<u>Taylor</u>

The days melted into each other, like a dream where everything is rainbows and ice cream, where everything is blooming flowers and big puffy clouds that look like sheep or angels or butterflies.

But two weeks later, feeling low, I slowly made my way to that rec room.

Wearing threadbare jeans and bare-chested, he sat on the table, his guitar on his lap as he strummed a vague melody accompanied by his mumbled voice.

I watched him a long moment as he concentrated on his music, locks of thick black hair falling over his handsome face. His fingers moved effortlessly over the frets. He made it look so easy.

Finally, he stopped and looked up. "Hey," he said with a smile. "Have you been standing there long?"

"Long enough to hear that," I said, trying to hide my emotions. "Sounds nice."

"What's wrong?" he quickly said as he set the guitar down behind him on the table.

I shrugged.

"I know you, Tay." He hopped off the table and came to me. "What's going on?"

"I didn't make it."

"Huh?"

I looked at him, trying so damned hard not to cry. It was a silly thing to cry over.

"The contest," I muttered. "I didn't make it to the next level."

"Oh, honey," he cooed as he swiftly pulled me into his arms and held me tight. "My little Tay. Those idiots don't know what they're doing."

Born Rotten
(A Married in Malibu Novella)

With my face buried in his chest, I wrapped my arms around his waist and held him as I shook my head.

"I can't believe it, Tay," he said as he forced me to look up at him. Laying a gentle kiss on my lips, he looked at me with that determined look he got whenever things didn't work out like he'd planned. "I'll go talk to whoever's in charge. I'll change their minds. I'll make them see the error of their ways."

I smiled. "You can't do that, Dex. Besides, I want to win this thing on my own merits… not because the judges were coerced.

"I bet the winner is like the kid of one of the judges or something."

I laughed and shrugged. "Maybe. Either way, it's all behind me now."

He ran his thumb under my eye, collecting a tear. "Clearly, it's not all behind you. I've never seen you so upset."

I let out a loud guffaw. "Oh really? You should have seen me when I walked out of the principal's office that first day when I met you."

"Ouch," he said with a grimace. "Don't remind me. I could kick myself for being such an ass." He pulled my face close to his. "I'll do anything to make it up to you. It pains me that I hurt you. That I could ever hurt you." He kissed me softly and then more passionately. "God, I love you."

Looking into his eyes, I realized just how quickly he'd actually managed to make me feel better. I smiled.

"I hope that you know that, even if you didn't win this thing, your poem is still a really great poem."

"Right. And you're not biased at all, are you?" I said with a teasing grin.

"Well, maybe... a bit... but that doesn't mean that it's not true. Maybe you just need to bring it to a different audience, one that will appreciate the profoundness of your words."

I smiled at Dex. "Profoundness?"

Dex grinned. "Wrong word choice?"

"No, perfect. You've come such a long way, Dex, from the first day we met to now. Pretty soon, you won't need me to tutor you anymore. You'll need someone else to help you move to the next level."

Dex shook his head and pulled me tight into his chest. "You're the only one I need. Just you, Tay. Just you."

Chapter 11

<u>Taylor</u>

Later that night, as I sat down to dinner with my parents, I thought of the contest and what it meant.

I wasn't meant to be on the path to become a poet…to be someone artistic. My talents was elsewhere, and I should be pursuing my talents wholeheartedly. Not engaging in some whimsy.

"You're awfully quiet tonight," my father said.

"I've come to a decision," I said as I set down my fork and knife.

"Oh?" Mom said. "About what?"

"My future. I've decided to go to med school. I'm going to be a doctor."

Born Rotten
(A Married in Malibu Novella)

While my father smiled with pride, there was concern in his wise eyes. "Is this what you really want?"

"Yeah," Mom said. "I thought you said you wanted to be a writer."

"That was just a wild and unrealistic dream," I said. "I need to plan for something real… something that's actually going to pay the bills."

"Well," Dad said. "You're certainly smart enough to get through med school."

"I've been looking at a few schools in the area," I said.

"Good," Mom said. "That means you can stay here while you get your degree."

I smiled at her and thought of Dex. Was he the real reason that I wanted to stay close by?

He called me the next day. "There are a few job openings near the campus where you'll be going."

"What are you saying?"

"I want to stay close, Tay. You'll go off to be a doctor and I'll work to pay for an apartment, and we'll be good."

"Dex..."

"And I've been looking at colleges," he went on. "Of course, I'm not looking at universities like you, but a junior college and, you know... we could live together... get married when you finish."

"I think you're looking at this through rose colored glasses, Dex. College is tough, and med school even tougher. It's time consuming. And I really want to be a good student... the best. We're talking about years and years. I'm not going to be able to see you much throughout all that."

"What are you talking about? Of course we can see each other. I mean, you'll have to eat meals, and you'll have to sleep at some point. I'm not saying that we'll be together all the time, but..."

"It won't work, Dex," I said. "These past months of being with you... I've seen a drop in my grades. I've let my heart take over my brain and I can't let that happen any longer."

"Tay. What are you saying? What are you telling me?"

"I'm telling you that our paths crossed, and it's been wonderful, but now our paths are leading us in different directions."

"No they're not."

"Yes, Dex. They are."

"I love you, Tay…"

"Don't make this any harder than it already is."

"We're meant to be together."

"That's a dream. It's only a dream… a dream that will never come true."

"You're wrong, Tay."

"Goodbye, Dex."

"No!"

With tears streaming down my cheeks and dripping all over my lap, I hung up.

Chapter 12

<u>Dex</u>

Taylor's words echoed in my head. I stared at my phone, unable to believe that she had just ended us. It didn't make sense. I immediately tried to call her back but got no response.

"What are you doing, Tay?" I said to my phone. "Did your parents put you up to this? Did you pastor dad force you to do this?"

But my phone remained silent, leaving me confused and angry.

I thought about the poem she'd read me; the poem that hadn't won the contest in which she'd entered. Did that have anything to do with this? Was she ashamed of having lost?

Born Rotten
(A Married in Malibu Novella)

No. It didn't make sense. None of it made sense.

I didn't see her in school the next day, and she didn't show up for our tutoring session. A sense of desperation gripped me.

It took three days for me to finally catch up to her and corner her in the stairwell of the school.

"Taylor," I said as I grabbed her hand.

"Don't do this, Dex."

"Do what? Try to figure out what's going on?"

"Dex…"

"Just tell me what's going on. You can't just leave me hanging like this."

"I'm sorry," she said. "You're right. It was very unprofessional of me to just drop you as a student."

"That's not what I'm talking about, and you know it."

"We'll start up again on Monday," she said, ignoring my comment.

"I don't understand, Taylor," I said, searching for an explanation. "Does this have to do with the poetry contest? Do you no longer believe in yourself? It drives me nuts to think that you could be giving up on your dream. And you've given up on us, too."

With a firm hand to my chest, she pushed me back and looked me square in the eyes. "I'll see you Monday after school for your tutoring session."

I had no choice but to step back and let her go.

The weekend was long and torturous as I awaited Monday. Never in my life had I been so eager for a weekend to pass and for Monday to arrive.

I was ready. That Monday, after class, I waited for her on the steps to the church. In the distance, I spotted her, coming, slow… almost reluctant… like she didn't really want to come.

My heart sank.

"Hi," I said when she finally reached me. I got up to face her, leaning in for the greeting kiss that had become our habit.

But she gracefully dodged it.

"I thought we'd take a look at history today," she said in a very formal, almost cold manner

I nodded and led her to my apartment. My defenses went up, slowly, a bit by bit, but they were there, getting ready, preparing. The old brooding, unhappy Dex was making a comeback and I didn't want to let him in. I'd come to like the happy Dex.

"Can I get you something to drink?" I said as she settled into the armchair and got her books out. "Water? Orange juice? Milk?"

"No, thank you."

I sat on the sofa and looked at her, trying to catch a glimpse of the Taylor I'd fallen in love with.

"Since you have a lot of catching up to do, we're going to be looking at industrialization today," she said.

Fine.

"And if we have time, we can even get into the global economics."

Fine.

I sank back into the sofa, sulking as she went through events that held absolutely no interest to me.

Ten minutes in, when she paused to check her notes, I leaned forward. "I love you, Taylor. If nothing else, you at least owe me a bit of an explanation. What did I do? What didn't I do?"

"It's over, Dex. It's just over because it should have never begun." She slammed her books closed, shoved them back into her bag and stood.

"Don't go," I said… almost begging.

"I was asked to tutor you," she said, holding her chin high. "I'm your tutor… and to a degree, I enjoy being your friend. That's all. Please don't torture us both with questions and longings for something more."

She turned and walked out, not even looking back.

I closed in on myself. My jaw tightened, and I fought back the burning tears that threatened to stream down my face. Clenching my fists, I turned away from the door and paced the living space of the small apartment.

I was right back where I'd always been... abandoned... and with no offer of an explanation.

"If that's the way you really want it," I muttered. "Fine. That's the way it will be."

*****

With the end of the school year around the corner, I was surprised to learn that I was actually going to graduate. While I'd avoided Taylor the last few weeks, I nonetheless wanted to thank her for all she'd done for me.

But when I saw her coming down the hall, her jaw still tight, her eyes averted… Fuck it.

"Hey, man," Beaver said as he came up behind me and clapped me on the shoulder. "A few of us are getting together to jam tonight. Want in?"

He'd caught me playing guitar one day on the church steps and we'd struck up a conversation. He, too, was a musician and we'd hit it off. It'd led to meeting a few of his buddies… it was cool to feel like I was a part of something.

"Sure," I said. "That'd be cool. Where?"

"Deter's place. You know where he lives?"

"Yeah. Cool. See you then."

In working to get Taylor out of my mind, I'd thrown myself into my music. In the past week alone, I'd written six songs. While I still had some work to do on them, the guts of each song was there… and it was strong.

Born Rotten
(A Married in Malibu Novella)

With my electric guitar case in hand, I arrived at Deter's place hoping to put some life into one of those songs.

"Hey, Dex," Beaver said as he idly thumbed his bass.

"Good to see you again," Deter said, twirling a drumstick between his fingers.

As I opened my guitar case and pulled out my old Gibson, I noticed a pretty blond girl, all dolled up in the latest fashion, sitting in a beanbag chair in the corner sucking on a bright pink lollipop. She offered me a small wave as I plugged in my guitar, and I responded with a nod.

"What are we jamming, man?" Beaver said.

"I have something I want to try," I said. "Are you guys familiar with the Aeolian mode?"

"Sure," Beaver said. "Not usually my style, but that's cool."

"In C." I played a succession of notes to lead the way. Soon, Beaver joined in and Deter followed with a gentle beat.

We went through the verse and chorus and then I finally added my voice. The words flowed through me. I knew them by heart. I'd known them all my life. Words of pain and heartache and frustration and anger. My guitar wept for me and as the song went on, Beaver upped the tempo, adding a new dimension that Deter quickly adopted.

By the time we ended the song, I was drained.

The pretty blond in the corner stood and looked at me.

I recognized her. I'd seen her before in school. In fact, Taylor had even suggested that I befriend her. 'Her father is in the music industry,' she'd said.

"That was quite a haunting performance," the blond said.

"I guess I'm in a haunting mood," I shot back.

Born Rotten
(A Married in Malibu Novella)

"I'm Britney Bailey," she said as she held out her hand.

I briefly shook her hand. "Dex. Dex Halliwell."

She nodded. "Yeah. I know. I've seen you around."

Wearing a bright pink crop top with yoga style black shorts, she was the complete opposite of Taylor. She was bubbly and outgoing and overtly sexy.

Funny. Months earlier I would have definitely gone for the popular girl like Britney without even giving Taylor a second glance. Even Taylor had pointed out how Britney was more my type.

Such a strange comment for her to make.

But, while Britney was a pretty girl, she wasn't Taylor.

"I like your voice," Britney said. "Different. Very interesting."

"Thank you."

"Let's do it again," Beaver suggested.

"Yeah," Britney said as she looked at me with a degree of confidence that I wasn't accustomed to. "I'd like to hear it again."

She returned to her beanbag, and we played the song again and again. By the end of the evening, the haunting ballad had morphed into a strong and emotionally driven rock song.

As I packed up my guitar, Britney came to me.

"I wasn't just saying that to be nice, you know," she said.

"What do you mean?"

"The comment about your voice," she said. "I'd love to hear more of your music."

I smiled and tried to convince myself that her interest in me was good. It was exactly what I needed to help me forget about Taylor.

And as the days went on and I spent more and more time with Britney, I grew quite fond of her.

Born Rotten
(A Married in Malibu Novella)

But she just couldn't replace Taylor. I hugged her and thought of Taylor. I kissed her and thought of Taylor. I fucked her and thought of making love to Taylor.

"There's something that I've been holding back on," Britney said one afternoon as we sat on the steps of the church, very much the way I'd often done with Taylor.

"What's that?" I said, running my fingers through her thick blond curls.

"When I say that I enjoy your music, it's not just from a whimsical sort of way."

Frowning, I tried to grasp what she was saying.

"I really think that you have something special, Dex," she went on. "And I think the world would enjoy discovering that something special."

"Well, it certainly is what I hope to do someday."

"My dad is a music producer," she blurted out. "I think it's time that you meet him."

Her father turned out to be a big, hefty guy with a well- trimmed beard and a crown of thinning white hair that stood on end.

"Nice to meet you, Dex," Mr. Bailey said as he nearly crushed my hand with his handshake. "Britney tells me that you're brilliant. Let's hear what you've got."

We were in the middle of their lavish living room which sat in the middle of their huge and lavish mansion which sat on acres of beautiful meadows and endless mountains.

I played him a few songs as he sat back and listened, stone-faced. After the third song, I stopped and waited for a comment… anything.

"Interesting," he said simply. "I'll see what I can do."

As I walked out of the mansion with Britney hanging onto me, I couldn't help but think of Taylor and of her desire to set me up with Britney. Had this been her plan all along? That I hook up with Britney, meet with her music producer father and get my career off the ground?

Then it suddenly hit me. Was that her reason for breaking up with me?   I shuddered at the thought.

"Are you okay?" Britney said as she opened the door to her baby blue sports car.

"Yeah," I said, suddenly feeling the need to get home.

She drove me back to the church, chattering all the way about how her father would make me a star, but I remained silent, lost in my thoughts. When we reached the church, she shut off the engine and was about to get out.

"Not tonight," I said as I got out of her car.

"I thought you'd want to celebrate," she said. "After all, this is the start of something big for you, Dex."

"You're right," I said, looking for a way to be alone without offending her. "And it's rather overwhelming. Give me the night to get my emotions in order. I'll see you tomorrow."

The next week was a blur as I hooked up with Britney but was left feeling cold every time. I tried to become interested in her. I tried to see all the advantages of dating someone like her… but the love just wasn't there.

By the time graduation day came around, I was more confused than ever. I arrived at the auditorium where the ceremony was to be held early, hoping…

Yes. There she was. Early, just like I knew she'd be.

"Taylor," I said as I cautiously came up to her.

Wearing her cap and gown, she was every bit the worthy student that she'd always been. Cute, regal, classy… smart.

Born Rotten
(A Married in Malibu Novella)

"Dex," she said, genuinely surprised to see me.

"I wanted to congratulate you," I said. "I heard that you're the valedictorian."

She nodded. "Yes. I am… and I'm a bit nervous about it," she said with that cute and humble smile that I loved so much.

"You'll do great," I said, sensing the well of emotions that was about to burst.

Looking at her, I realized just how much she cared about me, about my future… enough for her to give up the relationship that we'd had.

"I'd better go," she said quickly as others began to arrive.

I stood there numb as I watched her walk away, then turned to find my seat.

The auditorium quickly filled up and the ceremony was under way. The principal spoke as did a few other school officials… and then it was Taylor's turn.

She stepped up onto the stage and stood before the microphone.

"Our futures," she began. "Uncertainty. Unknown. It can be so scary and intimidating. But we're a resilient bunch, aren't we?"

The crowd nodded and as she went on, I was filled with pride. As much as it hurt to have lost her, I was proud to have known her, to have been a part of her world, and to have had her in my life.

The crowd suddenly burst into enthusiastic applause as she finished speaking. Like everything she did, she exceled as a speaker.

All I could think of throughout the remainder of the ceremony was getting a chance to talk to her. I just wanted to talk to her, to tell her how proud I was of her. But most importantly, I wanted to tell her that I still loved her.

That no matter how I tried, I can't forget her.

But as everyone started to scramble around, Britney came up and hooked her arm in mine.

Born Rotten
(A Married in Malibu Novella)

"Hey, baby," she said in that possessive way that had become her habit. "Come on. My friends want to meet you."

I looked past her to where Taylor was getting congratulatory hugs from her friends and family.

"Give me a minute, will you," I said as I squirmed out of Britney's hold.

I managed a few steps toward Taylor. Her parents were smiling at her, so proud. I got a few steps closer, and she briefly glanced up at me. Her eyes widened with alarm, and she gave me a slight shake of her head.

Gulping in a shattered breath, I stopped and just watched her. No one knew that we'd dated. No one knew how much I loved her. Her parents had no idea that we'd been passionate lovers.

And they never would. For Taylor's sake, I would keep this secret between us.

"Hey, baby," Britney said as she came up behind me and wrapped her arms around my waist.

She then wiggled her way around and under my arm. "Where you heading off to? Come on. My friends are waiting."

"I was just…" I couldn't tear my eyes off Taylor.

"Dex," Britney whined. "You're embarrassing me. Now, come on."

She looked up at me as she leaned into me. Catching the direction of my gaze, she looked at Taylor and back at me. "Dex?"

"Yeah," I muttered as I turned away from Taylor and brought my attention to Britney.

"Don't ever do that to me again, Dex," Britney muttered through her teeth as she led the way to her friends.

"Do what?" I said, confused by the anger in her voice.

She stopped suddenly and turned to face me. "You know exactly what you did. You walked away from me. We were celebrating this big day, and you walked away, leaving me embarrassed and alone. Then you go off to look at some girl… some nerdy girl. What the fuck?"

"You're making a big deal out of nothing, Britney," I said, holding back on the growing anger that was building up. "I just wanted to say goodbye to a friend."

Huffing, she glared at me. "I'm telling you, Dex. If you ever do that to me again…"

I forced a smile and tried to resume walking, but she stayed firmly in place.

"Dex," she said more aggressively. "I'm serious."

"I know you are."

"You know, my father is doing a lot to help you get your career off the ground. I assure you, you don't want to fuck around and make his daughter mad."

Frowning, I looked down at her. Had she just given me an ultimatum? Was she using her father as leverage that would allow her to throw a fit whenever she wanted to?

"I don't understand why you would bring that up. Besides, your father has no interest in the type of music that I want to make. He can't do much to help get my career off the ground… as you put it."

"He set you up with Derek Grolin, didn't he? Derek is one of the most prominent managers in the industry."

No. He wasn't. Derek Grolin was just barely getting his own career off the ground.

"After all I've done for you, the least you can do is to show me a bit of respect… especially when my friends are around."

It wasn't the first fight that we'd had regarding my 'respect' for her. Unwilling to let it get out of hand, I gently grasped her arm and turned her to head to her friends.

"I'll try to do better," I said gently.

"Well, I certainly hope so."

Born Rotten
(A Married in Malibu Novella)

That evening, we went out with her friends and as I sat there listening to them ramble on about various topics, I suddenly wondered what the hell I was doing there?

While Britney was a beautiful and outgoing girl who could be a lot of fun, her dark side had begun to pierce through the pretty wrapper. She was spoiled and could be mean and cruel when things didn't go her way.

As proven that night when I prepared to leave the gathering.

"I don't think that this is working out," I said.

She shrugged. "I know it's not fun for you to hang out with a group of women. Next time bring your buddies."

"That's not what I'm talking about, Brit. You and me. This isn't working. I need…"

"Fuck you!" she quickly shot back. "Don't you dare tell me that you need anything. I've given you everything you could possibly need."

I didn't want to argue. "I'm sorry."
I quickly turned and walked away.

Chapter 13

<u>Dex</u>

College wasn't really my scene, but I tried to make the most of it. I took a business class and essentially put my music aside. At night I worked at a convenience store, then got a better paying job as a security guard.

It was only after I graduated that I picked up my guitar again. Rummaging through old notes, I came upon the poem that Taylor had written. The words instantly struck me… shook me, brought me right back to those days with her.

I settled in to put music to her words and made a demo.

"I think you'd like it," I said to my imaginary vision of Taylor. "You'd really like it."

I called Derek.

"Hey, Dex," he said, happy to hear from me. "What've you been up to?"

"I have a song," I said. "I'd like to see you."

"Sure thing. How about three o'clock this afternoon."

"I'll be there."

I was a mess as I spent the next hours listening and relistening to the song, wondering what Derek would say. Was it too sappy? Was it too cliché?

But when I finally sat down with him, he listened intently and smiled.

"Interesting," he said.

"Of course, it's just a simple demo… just me and my guitar."

"Yes. I noticed that. And it's one of the hallmarks of a great song… simple, exposing a great melody, unusual chord changes. On top of it, you have a very interesting voice. Deep and raunchy, but with an ability to go up there and hit some of those high notes with heartfelt emotion. You're not formally trained are you?"

"No," I said. "I'm not."

He nodded and squinted as he looked up at me all while tapping his thin fingers over his glass desktop. "There are a few guys I'd like to hook you up with."

"Yeah?"

"Yeah. You ever heard of Gabriel Blake?"

"I've heard the name. A bassist, right? Didn't he play with Head of Betrayal?"

"That's right. And William Cole?"

I chuckled. "He was the drummer of Hard Freeze until they broke up."

"Right again."

"So what do we call ourselves?"

"How about Born Rotten?" I said.

"Hey yeah, sounds good, man. How'd you come up with that?"

"It's what I was told my entire life until a girl came along and challenged me on it."

"Good story, man. Born Rotten it is!"

*****

Gabe, Billy and I were the perfect fit. They understood me and they believed in me. We threw ideas off each other, added a chord here and there, a bridge, a modulation… all to make one great song after another. Within six months of meeting them, we had an album's worth of music and we were in the studio. It was the perfect distraction for forgetting Taylor, forgetting that I've ever been so deeply in love. I threw everything into the band and in music.

And when our first single hit the airwaves, it became an instant hit. We set out on a tour, with more and more songs hitting it big. I sang with all my heart the way I saw Taylor sang at church. It became the only way I would ever sing.

Born Rotten
(A Married in Malibu Novella)

Music magazines called me one of the most original singer/songwriters to come onto the scene in a long time.

I'd hit it big... real big.

Throughout those years, however, Taylor haunted me. She was the one who got away.

And now, as I sat alone in my big house, the envy of so many struggling artists, I enjoyed my expensive sipping tequila and thought of her... of all the empty years without her, until three days ago... when she wanted to marry her Dr. Perfect... in this very house.

Taylor Rhee was now the doctor she had worked so hard to become and now she was going to get married to another doctor.

It had been 13 years since we saw each other at high school graduation, and she's going to get married in Malibu. At my house. There wasn't a clearer sign for me to get her back into my life and my heart again than this. Of all the places for her to pick to get married at, it had to be the Malibu house I had temporarily put up as a wedding venue. It had to be fate. My second chance. I just need to convince Taylor, it's me she should be with, not the other guy…

*** * * * ***

Find out what happens 13 years later with
Dex, Taylor, and some friends in

**Married in Malibu (Drama Diaries Series:
Standalone Grumpy Sunshine Romances #1)**

https://www.amazon.com/dp/B09TD82SKL

Born Rotten
(A Married in Malibu Novella)

About the Author Kailin Gow

From visiting Romania, ALA YALSA Award-winning and Million-Selling Author Kailin Gow was asked to write stories about vampires; visiting the Black Forest in Germany and seeing the castles of Europe inspired her to write fantasy; visiting Asia's mystical mountains inspired her to write action adventure and mythological dystopians. From her experience in college as a peer counselor and her volunteer work with women's shelters, she was inspired to write contemporary romance with social issues for women, new adults, young adults, and teens. Having faced adversity, including battling stereotypes and bullying, Kailin Gow has become a well-known speaker and influential figure in media. Her adventurous bold spirit has taken her around the world, where she has ridden on top of elephants through jungles, hand-fed sting rays, studied kung fu from a Shaolin Temple monk, and learned cooking from a celebrity chef. She is a USA Today Bestselling author and has been a #1 Amazon bestselling author over two-hundred times. Her Bitter Frost Series is in development as a TV Series, and her contemporary romance Loving Summer is set to become a feature film. An multi-award-winning filmmaker, director, and actress; Kailin's films have premiered at Cannes, Los Angeles, Rome, England, Paris, Korea, Japan, and even in India's Ministry of Culture.

Compelled to write her first fiction book because of 9/11, Kailin Gow now has over 400 fiction books published under Kailin Gow and various Pen Names in many genres. As a speaker and host, she has hosted international shows at the Pasadena Civic Auditorium, been a celebrity judge at beauty pageants, been a judge for writing contests, and hosted television series.   She was featured as an Indie Author Success Story on the homepage of Amazon.com for a month and is also included in Amazon's book called Transformations. She is the first Asian American to have been featured on Amazon's homepage as an Author Success Story, and the first to have sold over a million books.

Follow Kailin at:

Kailin Gow Romance Newsletter Sign Up
http://madmimi.com/signups/5d7494ecee0a46feaa5c7a60f8f152f1/join

Bookbub
https://www.bookbub.com/authors/kailin-gow

Amazon Author Page

https://www.amazon.com/Kailin-Gow/e/B002BMAEH4